Other Yearling Books by Patricia Reilly Giff
you will enjoy:

WATCH OUT! MAN-EATING SNAKE
FANCY FEET
B-E-S-T FRIENDS
ALL ABOUT STACY
THE MYSTERY OF THE BLUE RING
THE RIDDLE OF THE RED PURSE
THE SECRET AT THE POLK STREET SCHOOL
THE POWDER PUFF PUZZLE

YEARLING BOOKS/YOUNG YEARLINGS/YEARLING CLASSICS are designed especially to entertain and enlighten young people. Patricia Reilly Giff, consultant to this series, received the bachelor's degree from Marymount College. She holds the master's degree in history from St. John's University, and a Professional Diploma in Reading from Hofstra University. She was a teacher and reading consultant for many years, and is the author of numerous books for young readers.

For a complete listing of all Yearling titles, write to
Dell Readers Service, P.O. Box 1045,
South Holland, IL 60473.

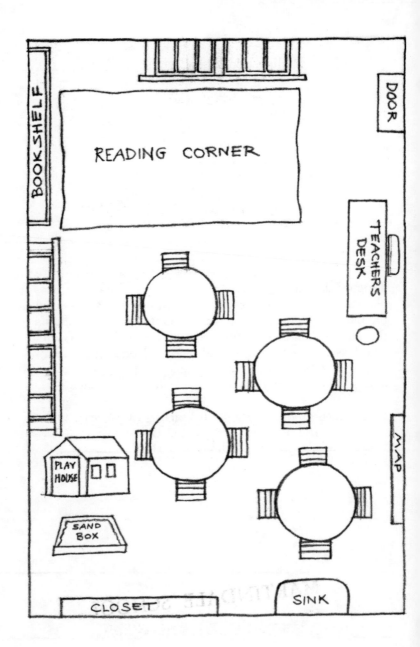

New Kids 5 at the Polk Street School

Spectacular Stone Soup

Patricia Reilly Giff

Illustrated by Blanche Sims

A YOUNG YEARLING BOOK

Published by
Dell Publishing
a division of
Bantam Doubleday Dell Publishing Group, Inc.
666 Fifth Avenue
New York, New York 10103

ISBN: 0-440-40134-8

Printed in the United States of America

January 1989

10 9 8 7 6 5 4

W

CHAPTER
1

Stacy Arrow hung her jacket on a hook.

Next to her Jiwon took off her coat.

Stacy pointed to a sweater on the floor. "Whose is that?"

"No one's." Jiwon shook her head. "It's been here all year."

"It looks like spinach," said Stacy. "Yuck green spinach."

"A spinach sweater," said Jiwon.

They started to laugh.

"Circle time," Mrs. Zachary called. "Chairs to the middle."

Stacy zoomed back to her seat.

She grabbed her chair and started to push.

Everyone else was pushing chairs too.

It sounded like thunder.

Stacy loved the noise.

Mrs. Zachary didn't, though. "Calm down," she said.

Eddie raced in front of Stacy.

"Beep," yelled Stacy.

She rammed into him.

"Hey," Eddie yelled.

Stacy gave him an I'm-sorry poke.

She turned around and zoomed down the aisle. She was going in the wrong direction.

Who cared? It was fun to race all over the room.

Then she remembered. She wanted to sit next to Mrs. Zachary.

Jiwon was on one side of the teacher already. Patty was racing for the other side.

Stacy gave her chair a push. Too late.

Patty zoomed into the best spot.

"I was here first." Stacy gave Patty a pinch on her blue-striped sleeve.

Patty shoved her chair into Stacy's ankle.

"Ouch," Stacy said.

"That's enough," said Mrs. Zachary.

Stacy bent down to rub her ankle. "Some friend you are," she told Patty.

"Is everybody ready?" Mrs. Zachary asked.

"I'm ready," said Stacy.

She turned so Mrs. Zachary couldn't see her.

She stretched her mouth wide.

She squished up her nose.

She stuck her thumbs in her ears. Then she waved her fingers.

"This looks like you," she told Patty.

Patty opened her mouth.

She let her tongue hang down.

"This looks like you," she told Stacy.

Stacy wiggled her nose.

"Give me back my Good Friends pin," Patty said.

Stacy made believe she hadn't heard.

She couldn't find Patty's Good Friends pin anyway. It was home somewhere.

She was wearing her A-1 Silver Shooter badge instead.

She had won it at a carnival.

At last everyone was in the circle.

"Let me look at all of you," said Mrs. Zachary.

Stacy sat up straight.

So did everyone else.

Mrs. Zachary liked to see straight-up children.

Stacy folded her hands in her lap.

So did Patty. That big copycat.

"This week we're going to do terrific

things," said Mrs. Zachary. She smiled at the class.

Stacy loved Mrs. Zachary's smile. She had thick white teeth. They stuck out a little.

Stacy stuck her teeth out a little too.

"We're going to talk about people helping people," Mrs. Zachary went on.

"That sounds good," said Eddie.

"I always help people," said Patty.

"Not always," said Stacy. She felt mean inside.

"You never help people," Patty said.

Stacy thought.

Patty was right.

She couldn't remember helping anyone.

Everyone began to tell Mrs. Zachary how they helped.

Twana had given her sister a penny.

Annie helped her grandfather in the backyard.

"I help my baby sister," said Eddie.

Stacy was sick of listening.

Mrs. Zachary kept nodding her head. "Spectacular."

Stacy looked down.

She wished she could think of something to say.

She'd love Mrs. Zachary to say "spectacular" to her.

She loved that word. It reminded her of stars and sparkles.

"This week I'll read helping-people books at story time," said Mrs. Zachary. "We'll draw lots of helping-people pictures too."

Eddie raised his hand. "I think it's time for snacks now."

"You're right." Mrs. Zachary laughed. "You never forget that."

Everyone started back to the tables.

Stacy didn't zoom this time.

She felt sad.

She was tired of not being friends with Patty.

She was tired of listening to how other people helped.

Then she had an idea.

She was going to help people right now.

She smiled at Patty.

She showed all of her teeth—even the ones in the back. Patty looked surprised.

Then she smiled too.

Wonderful, Stacy thought. She was turning out to be the best people-helper in the class.

Stacy let Eddie zoom his chair in front of her.

She let A.J. zoom too.

"Hey." She frowned a little. "You're supposed to say thank you."

Neither one of them heard her. They were racing to open their snack bags.

Stacy wanted to stick out her tongue.

She didn't, though. Perfect people-helpers never did stuff like that.

CHAPTER
2

It was Tuesday.

Stacy was standing in the pencil-sharpener line.

She was sick of waiting.

Eddie was taking forever.

"I'm trying to get the skinniest point in the world," he said.

"Story time," said Mrs. Zachary.

Stacy gave Eddie a poke. "Hurry up, will you?"

At last it was her turn.

She looked over her shoulder.

Mrs. Zachary was sitting in the old rocker.

The rest of the class was racing for the green story-time rug.

Stacy clicked her teeth together like a horse.

The pencil sharpener was filled.

She could hardly push her pencil into it.

Maybe she should clean the whole thing out.

Yes. It would be a great people-helper.

Mrs. Zachary would be thrilled.

The trouble was she didn't know how to do it.

"Is everybody ready?" Mrs. Zachary asked.

Stacy yanked the pencil sharpener. It came apart.

Shavings flew all over the place.

She brushed them into a pile on the floor.

She didn't want Mrs. Zachary to see.

She looked over her shoulder. Mrs. Zachary was rocking in her rocker. She was opening a big red book.

She wasn't paying any attention to the pencil sharpener.

Stacy looked at the sharpener.

Whew! Shavings all over it.

She picked it up with two fingers.

She tiptoed to the corner and shook it over the basket.

"I'm waiting, everybody," said Mrs. Zachary.

Stacy sped back to the window ledge.

She tried to fit the pencil sharpener back together.

It didn't work.

She tried again.

She looked over her shoulder.

Everyone was sitting on the green rug.

Stacy rubbed her hands on her skirt.

Suppose Mrs. Zachary found out she had broken the sharpener?

She went over to the green rug.

There was no room.

She had to sit on a tiny edge.

Her legs didn't even fit.

She tried to squeeze in a little.

"Oof," said Patty.

"Oof yourself," said Stacy.

"What's that stuff all over you?" Jiwon asked.

"Nothing." Stacy looked down.

Pencil shavings were stuck to her yellow shirt.

They were even stuck to her A-1 Silver Shooter badge.

She hoped Mrs. Zachary hadn't seen.

She brushed her badge.

She rubbed at her shirt. She could see a black smear on one sleeve.

Her mother would be ready to explode. Too bad.

She was ready to explode too.

"Now," said Mrs. Zachary.

She rocked her chair a little.

It made a soft squeaky sound.

Mrs. Zachary began to read.

Stacy looked over at the window ledge.

What would happen when Mrs. Zachary saw the pencil sharpener?

She'd explode too. "Pa-boom," Stacy said in a little voice.

"Are you listening?" Mrs. Zachary asked.

Stacy nodded. She knew all about the story.

Her sister Emily had told it to her one time.

So had her mother.

So had the librarian.

It was about soup.

Soldiers filled a pot with water. They didn't have anything else for the soup.

No cabbage.

No potatoes.

Nothing.

Then the soldiers dumped in a couple of stones.

Everyone began to help.

One man brought a carrot. Someone brought an onion.

The soup was filled with vegetables.

It was a pretty good story, Stacy thought.

It was too bad she had heard it forty-eight times.

It was too bad she was squished on the edge of the rug.

She sighed.

It certainly was too bad she had broken the pencil sharpener.

Mrs. Zachary closed the book. "Yes, indeed," she said. "Everybody helping one another."

She kept rocking. "Isn't that a lovely story?"

"Yes," the whole class said together.

"Yes, indeed," said Stacy.

"I have a great idea," said Mrs. Zachary. "Let's make stone soup."

"You're making me hungry," said Eddie.

Mrs. Zachary smiled. "We'll invite Ms. Rooney's class for Friday. They can share stone soup with us."

"We can make invitations," said A.J.

"Draw stone-soup pictures all over the place."

Stacy looked over at the pencil sharpener. "With crayons," she said. "Better than plain old pencils."

Mrs. Zachary stood up. "It will be spectacular. We'll start right now."

Stacy went back to her seat.

She hoped everyone would use crayons.

She hoped no one went near the pencil sharpener . . . otherwise she'd be in a lot of trouble.

CHAPTER
3

Stacy looked out the window.

She tried to think of a great invitation.

She tried to see if anyone was near the pencil sharpener.

Poor Mrs. Zachary.

Wait till she found out.

Stacy knew she'd be sad.

She'd be the only teacher in the whole school with no pencil sharpener.

Up in front Mrs. Zachary was putting words on the board.

Come	Ms. Rooney
Soup	Class
Invitation	Friday

Stacy didn't pay attention to the words.
She wasn't going to use words.
She couldn't read them anyway.
No, she was going to make pictures.
Spectacular orange pictures.

She'd draw them all over her invitation.

First she'd make an orange picture of Mrs. Zachary's class.

Then she'd do an orange Ms. Rooney's class.

Last she'd make a pot of soup.

Spectacular stone soup.

Maybe she'd make the soup green.

She didn't want it to look like tomato soup.

She hated tomatoes.

Just then Robert went past her table.

He began to root around in his cubby.

Robert was always doing that.

He never could find anything.

Stacy bet his crayons were lost.

He'd have to use a pencil.

He'd probably have to sharpen it.

He'd be yelling all over the place when he saw the broken pencil sharpener.

Poor Mrs. Zachary, Stacy thought again.

She stood up quickly. She went over to him.

"What are you doing?" she asked.

"Trying to find my crayons."

Robert's face was red.

He was pulling everything out of his cubby.

Old pictures.

Sloppy ones.

Two old snack bags. No wonder Robert was so skinny.

A pencil with no point.

Stacy clicked her teeth. "I knew it," she said. "I'll lend you a crayon."

Robert followed her back to her table.

He waited while Stacy picked up her crayon box.

It said EMILY ARROW on the front.

It was a good thing Emily didn't use her crayons much.

Stacy couldn't find her own crayons either.

She picked out a nice yellow one for Robert.

He shook his head. No.

"How about purple?"

"Uh-uh."

"Brown?"

"Yuck."

Stacy sighed. "Then what?"

Robert reached for the orange crayon.

"No good, Robert," Stacy said. "I need that."

"I like orange," he said. "I always use orange."

Mrs. Zachary stopped writing on the board. "All right," she said. "Let's get started."

Robert held out his hand.

Stacy slapped the yellow crayon into it.

Robert slapped it back on the table.

"Come on, Robert," said Stacy. "You heard Mrs. Zachary. Let's get started."

Robert looked as if he were going to cry.

Stacy thought about people helping people.

She thought about her invitation.

She thought about drawing a green Mrs. Zachary's class.

A blue one.

Yellow.

Robert was walking away.

He looked back. "Never mind. I'll use my pencil."

Stacy raced after him. "Big baby," she said. "Here."

She tossed the orange crayon on his table.

"Hey, thanks," he said.

Mrs. Zachary looked up. "What's happening?"

Stacy looked at Robert.

He'd tell Mrs. Zachary how nice she was.

He'd say Stacy had lent him her best pointy orange crayon.

Stacy began to smile.

She showed all her teeth . . . even the back ones.

Yes, indeed. It certainly was great to be a people-helper.

Robert didn't say anything, though.

He just slid into his seat.

"Get going," Mrs. Zachary said.

Stacy started back to her table. That was the last time she'd help Robert.

Let him use his old broken pencil for a change.

Then she remembered the sharpener.

She looked up.

Patty was heading straight toward it.

"Hey," said Patty. "Look at this."

Stacy didn't look.

She sat down at her table.

She stared at her invitation paper.

She knew what was going to happen next.

Yes.

Trouble.

CHAPTER
4

It was Wednesday.

"Today we'll give out the invitations," said Mrs. Zachary.

Stacy was glad Tuesday was over.

She was glad everyone had forgotten the pencil-sharpener business.

Everyone but her. Stacy Arrow.

Mrs. Zachary had snapped the sharpener together. One, two, three.

"What a mess," she had said. She shook her head at Stacy.

Stacy hated it when Mrs. Zachary shook her head.

She hated it most when Mrs. Zachary was shaking her head at her.

Right now Stacy pulled out her invitation. Her brown-and-green invitation.

She clicked her teeth.

She looked over at Robert.

She shook her head at him.

Robert was a real pain.

He had ruined her invitation.

Robert wasn't paying attention to her, though.

He was scribbling all over his paper.

Her orange point was flat.

She shook her head harder.

Up in front Mrs. Zachary was speaking. "Everyone in Ms. Rooney's class will be so surprised."

Stacy ducked her head.

Not everyone was going to be surprised.

No, sirree.

Her sister Emily was in Ms. Rooney's

class. And Emily was not going to be surprised. Not one bit.

Emily was a good guesser.

Too good.

Stacy had slipped a little.

She had told Emily there was a surprise.

"What kind?" Emily wanted to know.

"I'm not telling." Stacy put her hand over her mouth.

"Pretty please," said Emily.

It was hard to keep such a good surprise, Stacy thought. "Sharing." She kept her hand tight on her mouth.

Emily heard anyway. "Sharing what?"

Stacy opened two fingers so she could talk. "Food."

"Stone soup," Emily said. "We did that in Mrs. Zachary's class too."

Sometimes Emily was a pain.

She always got to do things first.

Right now everyone was yelling in the classroom. "Me. Me."

Stacy jumped.

She had forgotten where she was.

What were they yelling about?

"Me," she yelled too.

"I know someone in Ms. Rooney's class," said A.J.

"It's Room 113," said Twana.

The invitations, Stacy thought. Someone had to bring them to Ms. Rooney's room.

She should be the one.

"My sister is in that room." Stacy said it in a loud voice. She wanted to be sure Mrs. Zachary heard.

Mrs. Zachary was looking around.

"All right, A.J.," she said. "Take Robert with you."

A.J. marched to the front.

So did Robert.

They took the invitations.

Stacy slumped down in her seat.

No fair.

She never got to do anything.

She raised her hand.

"Can I get a drink of water?"

"May I." Mrs. Zachary nodded her head.

Stacy raced outside.

A.J. and Robert were fooling around in the hall.

"How about I take the invitations for you?" she asked them.

She smiled to herself.

What a nice people-helper thing to ask.

Besides, she'd get to say hello to Em-

ily. She'd say hello to her friend Beast
too. . . .

A.J. wasn't paying attention, though.

He was jumping from one tile to another.

Robert was jumping too.

"Too bad for you," Stacy said.

She bent over to get a drink.

She stood up with her mouth full.

"Watch out," A.J. yelled. "She's going
to get us with that water."

Just then a monitor came down the
hall.

It was a sixth-grade boy . . . the big
skinny one.

He was wearing an orange strap across his shirt.

He had on a gold monitor badge.

He had a cranky face.

"Hey, you," he yelled at Stacy and the boys.

The boys disappeared around the corner.

Stacy was caught. She swallowed as much water as she could.

Not all of it, though.

Some of it dripped down her neck.

"What are you doing in the hall?" the monitor asked.

"Getting water," said Stacy. "Helping

people give out invitations. Helping people, mostly."

He frowned. "Better get to your room before I report you."

Stacy started back.

She had never been reported.

She looked over her shoulder. "What happens when you get reported?"

"You're a fresh kid," he said.

Stacy raced into her classroom.

She'd have to ask Emily about being reported.

One thing she knew.

She never wanted that to happen to her.

CHAPTER
5

Stacy opened the big brown doors.

She was early today. Her father had driven her to school.

It was strange to be the first person there.

It was strange to be walking down the hall without Emily.

Emily was home with a sore throat.
Poor Emily.

Stacy looked around. It was hot in here with her raincoat on. It was hard to carry all her stuff by herself.

Stacy put down her snack bag.

She rested her soup onion on top of it. Her special stone-soup onion.

She took off her new yellow raincoat.

Whew, that felt better.

She straightened her shirt and rubbed her A-1 Silver Shooter badge.

Just then the doors opened. Two first grade boys came in.

They were talking and fooling around. They started down the hall.

They stopped when they saw Stacy.

They tiptoed past.

Stacy picked up her onion.

Two more kids came down the hall. "Watch out," one of them said. "There's the monitor."

"That's only a little kid," someone else said.

"Uh-uh," said the first one. "Look at the monitor badge."

Stacy looked down. They were talking about her A-1 Shooter badge.

She laughed a little hum-hum laugh.

"Quiet in the hall," she said.

Everyone was quiet.

Wow, Stacy thought.

She picked up her snack bag.

She waited for more children to open the big doors.

"No talking." She put on a cranky face . . . just like the sixth-grade monitor.

A girl with a ponytail went by.

She was hopping from one tile to the next.

"What's your name?" Stacy asked.

The girl looked scared. Maybe she thought Stacy would report her.

She had asked Emily what that meant.

It meant something terrible, Emily had told her. It meant tell the principal.

Stacy looked at the girl. "Don't worry. I won't report you."

The girl rushed away.

Stacy leaned back against the wall.

She knew she should go into Mrs. Zachary's room.

The monitor still wasn't there, though.

There was nobody to guard the hall. It was getting noisier and noisier.

Stacy spread out her arms.

She waved them around.

"Quiet in the hall." She yelled as loud as she could.

Yes, she thought. People helping people.

She was helping the teachers.

She was even helping Mr. Mancina, the principal.

Yes. Spectacular.

Just then the monitor came down the hall.

Stacy stopped waving her arms.

"You again?" the monitor asked.

He looked even more cranky than usual.

Stacy backed away from him.

She wanted to say she was just trying to help.

She was afraid, though.

She ran down the hall.

Her stone-soup onion rolled away from her.

She didn't stop for it.

She slid into Mrs. Zachary's room—and into the closet to hide.

She hid behind the spinach sweater.

Jiwon came into the closet. "What's the matter?" she asked.

"Ssh," Stacy said.

She was never going to be a people-helper again.

CHAPTER
6

Stacy scrunched down in her seat.

Suppose the sixth-grade monitor walked past?

Suppose he looked in the door?

He'd know where she was.

He'd report her.

Everyone else was up in front.

They were bringing things for the stone soup. They'd be ready to cook tomorrow.

Eddie had a bunch of carrots.

Twana had a potato.

Jiwon had some long green things.

She was waving them around in the air.

"Leeks," she told Mrs. Zachary. "Delicious."

Stacy scrunched down further in her seat.

She wondered where her onion was.

She didn't care, she told herself.

She wasn't going to be a people-helper anymore anyway.

If only she were home.

If only she didn't have to come back to the Polk Street School ever again.

She put her head on the table. Her eyes were burning.

She wished she had her lovely stone-soup onion.

Her mother said that onions were the best part of the soup.

No one else in the class had even thought of an onion.

Mrs. Zachary's class was going to have a terrible stone soup.

Mrs. Zachary clapped her hands. "Time

for gym," she said. "It isn't raining any-more. We can go outside."

Everyone went to the closet for jackets.

Stacy went too.

She had to get her raincoat.

She looked quickly. No bright yellow raincoat on the hooks.

None on the floor.

Everyone else was getting dressed.

Jiwon put on her red sweater with the white snowman.

She put her raincoat on top.

"My mother makes me wear a thousand things," she said.

Stacy kept looking for her raincoat.

Robert put on his tan jacket.

A.J. put on his blue sweater.

Everyone went to line up.

Everyone but Stacy.

She took a last look.

All that was left in the closet was the spinach sweater.

The horrible spinach sweater.

Stacy got in line.

Suddenly Stacy remembered.

She had left her raincoat in the hall.

Maybe it was still there.

Maybe not.

It was probably gone forever.

"Where's your coat?" Jiwon asked.

"It's lost," Stacy said.

She tried to look as if she weren't going to cry.

Jiwon opened her mouth. She looked sad for Stacy.

The class marched out the door.

Stacy was last.

She peeked out.

She wanted to be sure the monitor was gone.

The hall was empty.

No monitor.

No yellow raincoat.

No stone-soup onion.

Stacy marched down the hall.

Maybe she should hide in the girls' room.

It was freezing out.

She shook her head.

Mrs. Zachary would know she was missing.

Mrs. Zachary knew everything.

What would Mrs. Zachary say when she saw Stacy without a coat?

Stacy would say she was hot.

Very hot.

Spectacular hot.

Stacy closed her eyes for a minute.

She thought of her mother.

She couldn't tell her mother she didn't need a coat.

Her mother would know it was lost.

No one Stacy knew had ever lost a coat. Especially a brand-new yellow one.

The line stopped.

Stacy bumped into Robert.

She looked around him to see what was happening.

Mrs. Zachary had stopped.

She was talking with Ms. Rooney.

They were probably talking about the stone-soup party.

Whoosh. Jiwon dashed past her.

"Hey, Jiwon," yelled A.J. "You're going the wrong way."

Jiwon didn't stop.

She didn't even look back.

Stacy waited for the line to start again.

Mrs. Zachary was talking a long time.

Mrs. Zachary and Ms. Rooney liked to talk together. They were good friends.

Just then Stacy heard a noise.

It was Jiwon.

Her raincoat was unzipped.

It was flying behind her.

Underneath she was wearing the spinach sweater.

In her hand was the red sweater with the snowman.

She held it out to Stacy. "Put this on," she said. "It's freezing out."

Stacy opened her mouth.

Jiwon zipped her raincoat over the spinach sweater. She smiled at Stacy. "No one will see."

The line began to move.

Stacy pulled on the red sweater.

She wanted to tell Jiwon she was a people-helper.

A spectacular people-helper.

Mrs. Zachary put her finger on her lips, though.

They were passing the office.

Just then the office door opened.

It was the sixth grade monitor. "Wait," he yelled.

Stacy started to run.

She opened the big doors and raced outside.

CHAPTER
7

Today was the stone-soup party.

"Hurry," Jiwon told Stacy.

Stacy nodded. She hung up her just-for-fun fur jacket.

It was her best one.

She was glad it didn't fit Emily anymore.

Stacy reached into her pockets. She pulled an onion out of each.

Two onions were better than one.

After what had happened yesterday, Stacy wanted to be a people-helper.

A spectacular one.

Outside the closet everyone was running around.

Patty was putting chairs in a circle.

Robert had the paper cups.

Mrs. Zachary was up in front.

She was wearing a pink lace apron over her jeans.

She was stirring a huge pot of soup on a burner.

Stacy went up front too.

"Careful," said Mrs. Zachary. "It's hot."

Stacy held out her onions. "Is it too late for these?"

Mrs. Zachary smiled. "Stacy, it's never too late for onions."

"My mother says onions are the best part."

Mrs. Zachary took the onions. "Your mother is right. Let's chop them up."

Stacy sat on the edge of a chair to

watch. "Feeling happier today?" asked Mrs. Zachary.

Stacy nodded.

Mrs. Zachary patted her shoulder. "You're certainly a fast runner."

Mrs. Zachary was crying a little. "Onions make my eyes water."

"That's what my mother says too."

Stacy thought back to yesterday.

She had slammed out the big brown doors. She had raced across the yard.

"Stop," the monitor kept yelling.

"Run," yelled Jiwon.

"Come back, Stacy," Mrs. Zachary had called.

The gates were closed. Jim, the cleaning man, was trying to fix the lock.

Stacy raced around in a circle.

The monitor raced too.

"Go, Stacy," yelled A.J.

Stacy was out of breath.

She had a pain in her side from running.

The monitor reached out. He grabbed her shoulder.

"You lost your raincoat," he said.

Just then, Mrs. Zachary reached them. "What's the matter? What's going on?"

"Are you going to report me?" Stacy asked. She moved closer to Mrs. Zachary.

"I wanted to tell you. I found your raincoat. I left it in the office for you."

"Thanks," Stacy said.

The monitor smiled. "I was just doing my job . . . helping people."

At her desk Mrs. Zachary chopped the last bit of onion.

She wiped her hands on her lace apron.

"I'll put in the onions," said Stacy.

"Good girl," said Mrs. Zachary. She held the pot steady.

A.J. rushed past. "Smell those onions," he said. "I love onions."

Stacy smiled to herself. She had a surprise. She had worked on it all afternoon.

Just then the door opened. It was Ms. Rooney's class.

Dawn Bosco was carrying a big box of crackers.

"Let me at that soup," Stacy's friend Beast yelled.

"It smells like my mother's soup," said Emily.

"Oops." Mrs. Zachary looked around. "We don't have any napkins."

Stacy dashed to the closet.

She had napkins to give out. Tons of them.

She had drawn stone-soup pictures on them for the class.

Up in front Mrs. Zachary started to give out the soup.

Stacy stood in line.

She was starving!